Hating Mr. Wentworth

A Flirty Enemies-to-Lovers Romcom Between the Billionaire CEO She Swore to Hate and the Woman He Can't Resist

Hana York

PINK POP PUBLISHING

Hating Mr. Wentworth

(Don't Fall for a Billionaire Book 1)

Copyright © 2025 by Hana York

www.HanaYork.com

CONTENTS

Chapter One

LIZ

EVEN HIS NAME MADE my eye twitch.

Billy Wentworth the Third.

What self-respecting adult still went by *Billy*? Was *Trip* already taken?

I glared at the subject line in my inbox like it had personally insulted me:

Company Leadership Transition – CEO Introduction

The body of the email was bland corporate nonsense—vision, innovation, synergy—but the real message was clear: William Wentworth had passed the baton to his son.

And that meant my future now rested in the hands of some overprivileged, beer-pong-playing, ultimate-frisbee-throwing trust fund baby.

I scrolled past the glowing list of Billy's so-called accomplishments, which read less like a résumé and more like a LinkedIn fantasy crafted by overpaid PR elves. A European business school. "Strategic entrepreneurial ventures" (sure thing). A background in logistics, which probably meant *"my assistant booked all my flights."*

I was still scowling at the screen when a voice floated in from the doorway.

"So, how's it feel knowing our fate now rests in the hands of a guy who probably calls his buddies 'bro' unironically?"

I looked up.

Mia—best friend, product designer, chaos goblin—leaned against the doorframe, smirking. Sketchpad under one arm, pencil stabbed through her bun like a weapon.

I slumped back in my chair. "Infuriating. I work my ass off, and now Mr. Trust Fund with a private jet gets to decide if I'm worth keeping."

"He went to business school in Europe," she said, strolling in and dropping into the chair across from me.

"Which means he probably spent three years drinking overpriced espresso and calling it networking."

I snapped my laptop shut. "I've spent five years building this portfolio. Five years of skipped holidays and writing pitches in parking lots. And now some billionaire baby rolls in to 'evaluate' me like I'm a line item."

"Rumor is he's hot, at least."

I made a face. "I don't care if he looks like a Hemsworth and smells like fresh cinnamon rolls. I don't trust anyone handed that much money and power."

"No argument. But if he *does* look like a Hemsworth... maybe you flirt your way into a raise."

I groaned. "If I have to flirt to keep my job, I'm quitting and opening a waffle truck."

Mia lit up. "Do I get equity?"

"You're COO and Chief of Toppings."

"Perfect. I've been dying to test my s'mores waffle."

The corner of my mouth twitched. But then reality crept back in.

There was one glaring issue with my credentials I couldn't fix: the missing degree on my résumé. The one I should've had—if it weren't for the Bradley Situation.

The one thing *Billy* might notice.

My stomach turned. I straightened. "Whatever. I'll do what I always do—work twice as hard and leave zero room for doubt. If he wants to fire me, he'll have to actually find a reason."

Mia grinned. "And if he does, we'll key his yacht."

I laughed. "You think he has a yacht?"

"Billionaire playboy? It's practically issued at birth."

I leaned back in my chair, the humor fading.

I didn't need to meet him to know exactly who he was.

Rich. Polished. Entitled.

The kind of man who always came out on top—while girls like me were left cleaning up the mess.

"God, I hate him already." I muttered.

BRETT

I'd been at the office for less than an hour and already wanted a drink.

The conference room smelled like burnt coffee and desperation. A dozen executives sat stiffly around the table, faces split between forced enthusiasm and quiet panic. They wanted to impress me.

More accurately, they wanted to keep their jobs.

Couldn't blame them. My father had run this company into the ground, and now I was the one tasked with dragging it out of its financial grave. That meant figuring out who was actually pulling their weight—and who was just here for the catered lunches and quarterly bonuses.

An older exec leaned forward, clasping his hands like we were about to exchange state secrets.

"We're all eager to hear your vision, Billy. Where do you see the company in five years?"

"Brett," I corrected smoothly.

He blinked. "That's what I said... Brett."

"No, you didn't." I kept my voice even, though this was the *third* time someone had called me Billy since I walked in.

My legal name might be William Wentworth III, but I'd gone by Brett since college.

The nickname 'Billy' was my dad's idea of legacy.

And it wasn't one I planned to inherit.

The entire table shifted uncomfortably. I could practically hear the internal Post-Its being stuck to their brains: Not Billy. Brett. Do not screw this up!

And then—

A snort.

Quiet. Sharp. Definitely not imaginary.

My gaze locked on the source.

Blonde curls. Blue eyes. Curves that made my focus wobble.

She didn't look away. Didn't apologize. Just lifted one perfectly arched brow like I was wasting her time.

I didn't know who she was, but I knew exactly what that look meant.

She'd already written me off.

Another rich boy in a tailored suit who thinks "work ethic" is a brunch spot.

One look and I knew—she already had a nickname for me, and I wasn't going to like it.

I looked away first.

Not because I was rattled. Definitely not.

It would take more than a curvy blonde with attitude and a glare sharp enough to draw blood to shake me.

I just had a meeting to run. That was all.

Totally professional.

Totally unaffected.

I straightened my tie. "As for your question? It's simple. We're going to stop hemorrhaging money and start innovating again."

I let the words settle. Felt the collective pulse in the room stall.

"Bright Spark used to lead the industry in educational play. Now we're recycling the same stale ideas while our competitors eat our lunch."

Silence.

Not passive. Not polite.

Heavy. Weighted. Like everyone was trying not to look guilty.

A few executives glanced down at their folders—probably filled with the exact recycled trash I was talking about.

"Over the next two weeks, I'll be meeting with each department. Come prepared with data, not excuses."

I stood and buttoned my jacket.

"Meeting adjourned."

Chapter Two

BRETT

As the room cleared, I noticed the blonde lingering.

She moved slowly—deliberately—like she was waiting to pounce.

Great. Exactly what I needed before my first coffee had fully kicked in.

"Something on your mind?" I asked once it was just the two of us.

She looked up, eyes locking with mine. Cool. Unflinching. Blue as hell.

"Not at all, *Brett*."

The way she said my name dripped with sarcasm.

"You disagree with something I said?" I asked, more curious than I should've been. Most employees were still walking on eggshells. She looked like the kind of woman who'd argue with you, win, and still make you wish she hadn't walked away.

She tilted her head slightly, eyeing me like I was something unpleasant clinging to the bottom of her shoe.

"Nope. Just fascinated by how confidently you talk about innovation for someone who's been here, what—five minutes?"

Ah. So that's how this was going to go.

"I did my homework," I said, keeping my tone even. "And if my confidence bothers you, the next few weeks might be rough."

Her mouth twitched.

"Good thing I have a high tolerance for mansplaining," she said sweetly.

Then she smiled—the kind of smile that dared me to keep talking so she could shred me again.

I should've walked away.

I didn't.

Instead, I crossed my arms and leaned casually against the table—because, for some reason, I suddenly wanted to get a rise out of her.

"Should I be flattered, or are you always this hostile before noon?"

"Depends on the level of entitlement I'm dealing with before my second coffee."

That one landed.

I straightened slightly. "So you've already decided I'm an overpaid idiot with no clue what I'm doing?"

"Your words, not mine," she said with a shrug, gathering her folder.

I couldn't help it—I laughed. She was refreshingly honest. Everyone else in this building was either kissing my ass or walking on eggshells. This woman looked like she'd rather eat glass than pretend to be impressed by my last name.

Her eyes narrowed at my laugh, like I'd just failed some test.

"I'm glad you find this entertaining," she said. "Some of us have actual work to do."

"And you are...?" I asked, realizing I still didn't know her name.

She straightened to her full height—which wasn't much, even in those heels that made her legs look endless.

"Elizabeth Bentley, Senior Account Executive." She didn't offer her hand. "Most people call me Liz."

"Liz," I repeated, testing the name. It suited her. Short, sharp, no room for bullshit. "I've heard good things about your work."

She blinked, thrown for a half-second before her shields went back up. "From whom, exactly? You've been CEO for all of twenty minutes."

"Quarterly reports. Client retention data. Your name came up in my research." I wasn't lying. I'd spent weeks poring over every file, every report, every piece of data I could get my hands on. "You consistently outperform every other account executive."

Her chin lifted slightly. "I know."

She tucked the folder under her arm and turned toward the door, pausing just long enough to toss over her shoulder, "Well," she said with a bright, fake smile. "Welcome to Bright Spark, *Brett*. Can't wait to see your leadership in action."

God, she was impossible. All sharp edges and stubborn pride, clearly determined to hate me on principle.

So why the hell was I enjoying this?

Why was I still standing there, thinking about the way she said my name—like it was a curse and a dare wrapped in one?

This woman?

She was going to be a problem.

And I couldn't wait.

LIZ

I stormed into Mia's workspace without knock-ing—which was fine because she never knocked on mine either.

Her desk was a disaster zone of sketches, clay molds, and three different coffee cups in various stages of abandon-ment. She was hunched over her sketchpad, completely absorbed—until she looked up and caught sight of my face.

"Uh-oh," she said immediately. "Who pissed you off this time?"

"That would be Billy," I said sweetly. "I mean—*Brett*. Apparently, we're all supposed to pretend he's not a third-generation billionaire baby now that he's using his *'Serious Adult Name'.*" I added air quotes for emphasis.

Mia's eyebrows rose. "So? Was he as much of a douchebag as you imagined?"

"Worse. So much worse." I dropped into the chair across from her with a dramatic sigh. "He looked like the kind of guy who'd roll in from a yacht party—six-foot-four, broad shoulders, obnoxiously perfect brown hair, artfully tousled like he'd just woken up from a nap in a private jet."

Mia made a face. "Ew. So, infuriatingly hot?"

"Unfortunately, yes," I grumbled. "And he had the nerve to leave the top button of his shirt undone, like full professionalism was just a suggestion. Add that to the tailored navy suit, the smug look, and the tie he probably loosened for effect, and it's practically a walking billboard. One that says: 'I inherited this company and a yacht'."

"You sound... flustered."

"I'm furious," I corrected.

Mia raised an eyebrow but said nothing.

"He thinks he's clever," I said, gesturing wildly like I was presenting closing arguments on *Law & Order: CEO Unit*. "All calm and smug, with his rolled-up sleeves and his 'I'm not like other billionaires' energy."

Mia's head snapped up, eyes wide. "Did he actually say that?"

"No," I snapped. "But he radiates it. Like he thinks because he doesn't wear a Rolex or say 'synergy' every five minutes, we'll all forget his last name is Wentworth."

And then there was the way he looked at me—deep brown eyes fixed on mine, like I was a puzzle he was already bored of solving. And the way he said my name? Slow. Smug. Like he was rolling it around in his mouth just to see how it tasted.

Mia flipped her pencil and made a minor correction on her sketchpad. "Did you tell him that?"

"Of course not. I was professional."

She paused. "Define professional."

I flopped back in the chair, arms crossed. "I may have implied he was a mansplaining egomaniac with a God complex."

Mia blinked. "Wow. Subtle."

"Ugh. He's the worst."

"Uh-huh," she said, still sketching.

I squinted at her. "What?"

She gave me a look. The kind of look that usually came with a warning siren and a flashing red light.

"So. You're obsessed with him."

I scoffed. "I hate him."

"Same thing."

"It is not the same thing. *Obsessed* implies I think about him constantly. I just want to make sure he doesn't destroy the company I've spent five years building. He's exactly the kind of guy who never had to try. The kind who thinks the world bends to his will because it always has."

"Mmm-hmm." She flipped a page. "Totally normal amount of rage-rambling about someone you don't care about."

"I'm venting! The meeting just happened!"

Mia tilted her head. "Uh-huh."

I sat up straighter. "Anyway, he had the nerve to tell me he'd 'heard good things' about my work. Like he's been studying up on all of us."

Her eyes flicked again, now fully intrigued. "Wait. He knew who you were?"

"Said he read the quarterly reports. Claims my name came up in his 'research'." I did air quotes again. "Like he actually combed through our client retention data."

But a tiny voice in my head whispered... *what if he had?* And why did that make my stomach do a weird little flip?

Mia grinned like the Chesire Cat. "Sounds like somebody met her match."

"He's insufferable."

"You're one printer jam away from hate-kissing him in the copy room."

"I would rather kiss an actual printer."

"That would void the warranty," Mia said with a smirk.

"At least the printer is honest about its intentions. It doesn't pretend to be something it's not."

"Kinky," Mia said, wiggling her eyebrows.

I stared at her. "You're dead to me."

Chapter Three

BRETT

I DIDN'T SCHEDULE THE meeting out of spite.

It was strategy. Precision.

After the leadership debrief, I already knew who I wanted to start with.

Elizabeth Bentley.

She'd lingered in my head longer than I wanted to admit. That glare. The razor-sharp mouth. The way she said *Brett* like she'd invented sarcasm just for me.

I told myself it was because I needed to determine if she was an asset or a liability.

Not because I was curious.

Not because I'd wondered what it would take to crack that steel exterior and make her forget to hate me for five seconds.

It was business.

She walked into my office exactly on time. Not a minute early. Not a second late.

Composed. Controlled. But the tension in her shoulders gave her away—the kind of stiffness that said *I've practiced this calm, and I will not break character.*

"Ms. Bentley," I said.

She nodded coolly. "Mr. Wentworth."

I gestured to the chair. "Please."

She sat like it was a trap. Straight back, legs crossed, hands folded so tight they might fuse together. Immaculately professional. Except for the eyes.

Those were already daring me to try something.

I opened her file—not because I needed it, but because looking at paper was safer than looking at her. "Five years at Bright Spark. Started in entry-level marketing. Promoted to account exec in three years."

"Two," she corrected a little too quickly.

I glanced up. That flash of tension in her jaw—there it was again.

"Your client retention rate is ninety-two percent. Highest in the company."

Her posture loosened by half a degree. "I prioritize relationships."

"So do your clients, apparently." I flipped to the next page. "Parkwood Elementary's principal called you 'indispensable.' Said you're the only reason they renewed this year."

A flicker of pride slipped through. "They were working with a shoestring budget. I restructured their plan so they could still use our products without overspending."

"At the expense of your commission."

She didn't blink. "It was the right call. And it's brought in three new accounts. Worth it."

I leaned back. The file said high-performer. But this? This was fire. Passion, laced with something else. Conviction. Sharp-edged and unapologetic.

That kind of intensity was valuable. Also volatile. Especially when it was aimed directly at me.

I shut the file. "Tell me something I won't find in here."

Her eyebrow lifted. "Excuse me?"

"Something personal. Something that explains why you fight like hell for clients who can barely afford the shipping fees."

She paused. Clearly didn't like the question.

But she didn't dodge it either.

"I was a scholarship kid," she said. "My mom taught first grade and waitressed on weekends. I watched her stretch paychecks and still come up short."

Her voice didn't waver, but it was lower now. Realer. "These kits? These aren't just toys. Not to people like her. They're what kids remember. What keeps them curious."

I caught it then—how she leaned in slightly, just enough to forget the performance. Her voice softened. Her guard didn't drop, but it shifted. Like maybe she didn't really hate me. Just didn't trust me yet.

And then I did the thing I hadn't meant to do.

I flipped to the section of her file that didn't match the rest.

"Your résumé says Stanford," I said. "But your file doesn't list a degree. Is there a reason for the discrepancy?"

Her expression changed so fast it could've given me whiplash.

Her voice was ice. "I completed seven semesters. I didn't finish. Personal reasons."

I waited. Let the silence stretch.

She didn't elaborate.

I nodded slowly. "Didn't seem to impact your performance."

"No," she said, lifting her chin a fraction. "It didn't."

Her tone was sharp again, polished with practiced armor. Like she'd been asked that question too many times—and had learned exactly how to make people regret it.

Most people I'd met here were either terrified of me or overly eager to please.

She was neither.

She wasn't trying to win me over—she was trying to keep me out.

And that, somehow, made me want to know everything.

LIZ

I kept my expression neutral. Steady. Unbothered.

"Personal reasons," I said, letting the words hang between us.

He didn't push. Just gave a slow, measured nod.

And that was somehow worse.

The professional distance of his reaction felt like a trap—as if he were waiting for me to volunteer more information, to expose a vulnerability he could use later.

I'd spent five years proving myself, and I wasn't about to let Billy—Brett—Wentworth undo all that with one glance at my incomplete education.

"Your numbers speak for themselves," he said after a beat, closing the file.

I nodded once—tight, clipped. Then stood.

He stood too.

Because, of course he did. Polite. Proper. Predictable.

I hesitated for half a second.

Technically, he'd called this meeting.

But I was done.

"Thanks for your time," I said, and even to my own ears, it sounded like I was trying not to choke on it.

He nodded again, that unreadable face still giving me absolutely nothing.

I turned on my heel and walked out.

The door clicked shut behind me.

And just like that, the calm gave way.

Not a breakdown. Not tears. Just that hollow, sinking weight pressing on my chest—the kind that creeps in when you've worked so hard to outrun your past, and suddenly, it catches up.

I knew that feeling.

I knew it because of *him*.

The Bradley Situation.

Bradley was the golden boy at Stanford—charm, confidence, and trust-fund swagger in one perfectly tousled package. He wore entitlement like a custom suit and had a smile built to disarm.

And for a while, it worked.

He made me believe I belonged.

He made me believe someone like him could want someone like me.

He didn't, not really.

While I was pulling all-nighters and obsessing over every detail, he was copying my assignments word for word and submitting them as his own.

I didn't know.

Not until the university flagged the overlap and launched an investigation.

He denied everything. Said I was the one who copied him.

And they believed him.

Of course they did.

He was a legacy with a donor dad and a spotless record.

I was a scholarship kid—smart but expendable.

His father wrote a check and Bradley walked across the graduation stage in a designer suit.

And I?

I packed up my dorm room and disappeared—one class short of a degree.

I didn't tell anyone.

Not my mom. Not my friends.

I rewrote the ending.

Polished the résumé.

Smiled when I said I'd taken a job early.

And for a while, I convinced myself it didn't matter.

That it hadn't wrecked me.

But it had.

And that's why I don't trust charm, or confidence, or a pretty boy with a family name and a carefully curated backstory.

It's why I see someone like Brett Wentworth and I already know exactly who he is. Exactly *what* he is.

Because I've lived that story.

And I barely made it out the first time.

Chapter Four

BRETT

"Let me guess," Logan said, settling into the chair across from me like he owned it. "First day as CEO, and you've already terrified half the executive team."

I didn't look up from my bourbon. "Not quite half."

"Ah. So modest."

He lounged back, annoyingly relaxed in one of his ridiculous Hawaiian shirts. Logan Donovan was the human equivalent of charm on tap—CEO of his own boutique travel company, unreasonably well-liked, and irritatingly perceptive when it came to me.

"You're supposed to ease into power," he said, propping one ankle over his knee. "Shake some hands. Flash that smolder you pretend isn't smoldering. Toss out a few buzzwords—'agile,' 'growth hacking,' and 'vertical synergy.' You know. Foreplay."

"I'm not interested in foreplay," I muttered.

Logan raised a brow. "And now I'm concerned. What did she do to you?"

I froze.

He grinned. "Ah. There it is."

"I don't know what you are talking about."

"Bullshit. You've got that look on your face. All broody and wound-up. Like someone questioned your authority, and you didn't hate it as much as you should've."

I took a slow sip. "Her name is Elizabeth Bentley. Senior account exec. Sharp. Passionate."

"Oh God," Logan sighed, delighted. "You're intrigued. You *hate* being intrigued."

I didn't respond.

"She challenged you," Logan said, more seriously now. "That's rare. Most people walk on eggshells around you."

"She was defensive," I said. "Borderline insubordinate."

Logan gave a low whistle. "Now I really wish I'd been there."

I didn't respond. Just took another sip.

"Let me guess—she sized you up and handed your ego back with a smile."

Sometimes I really hated Logan.

***

I returned to the office after dinner because I had work to do—files to review, departments to assess, people to evaluate.

The building was mostly dark when I stepped off the elevator. Quiet. Still.

I wasn't expecting anyone else.

Which is why I stopped short at the light glowing at the end of the hall.

Liz's office.

Of course she hadn't left.

I walked toward her door, drawn by an inexplicable curiosity I didn't want to examine too closely. The door was partially open, and a sliver of warm light spilled into the hallway.

I paused at the threshold, about to knock—then froze.

She was bent over, reaching for something that had fallen next to her desk. Her pencil skirt had ridden up, hugging the curves of her ass and thighs as she stretched forward, one hand braced on her desk, the other extended toward the floor.

And yeah, I noticed her ass.

Curvy. Perfectly distracting. The kind of view that punched straight through logic and professionalism like a wrecking ball.

I dragged my gaze away.

Or tried to.

But my body didn't get the memo.

Something primal kicked in, sending blood rushing south with embarrassing speed. To my complete irritation, I was getting hard—right there in the goddamn hallway like some hormone-addled teenager.

I shifted, adjusting my stance. What the hell was wrong with me? This woman was argumentative, standoffish, clearly gunning for my head. I didn't even like her.

And yet... here I was, ready to worship the ground beneath her heels.

I cleared my throat loudly—partly to alert her, partly to regain control.

She jerked upright, spinning around with wide eyes that narrowed the second they landed on me.

"What are you doing?" she demanded, voice sharp with embarrassment—and something else. Something that made my pulse jump.

"I saw the light," I said, aiming for neutral. "Didn't think anyone else was burning the midnight oil."

Her cheeks flushed, but she didn't look away. "Some of us don't have the luxury of clocking out early."

That one stung more than I cared to admit.

"Is that what you think I do?" I asked, taking a step into her office. The air between us felt charged, static crackling with tension.

"Isn't it?" she challenged, crossing her arms. The movement pushed her breasts together slightly under her silk blouse, and I forced my eyes to stay locked on hers.

"No. Actually, I was having dinner with a friend before coming back to review department files."

Her arms stayed crossed, but her chin lifted, eyes blazing. No hesitation—just a challenge.

"Let me guess—you've already decided who stays and who goes. Just another rich guy playing king."

There it was. The crack.

The one she didn't mean to show.

I stepped closer before I could stop myself.

"I'm just trying to understand who belongs here."

She didn't flinch. Just lit up like a match.

"You don't know me," she snapped. "You don't know what I've done to get here. What I've given up. But you think you can sit in your glass office and decide if I'm worth keeping?"

"That's not what I—"

Before I could finish, she poked me.

Right in the chest.

Hard.

And I don't know what surprised me more—the fire in her eyes or the jolt that ran through me at her touch.

LIZ

I meant it to be a statement. A shove. A reminder that I wasn't afraid of him—or the ridiculous power he carried with that last name and pressed suit.

I didn't expect my finger to land on solid muscle.

Hard muscle.

Not polished-gym-bro muscle. Not soft-rich-guy-who-hires-a-trainer muscle.

No—this was the kind of solid that said he did the work. Earned it.

Shit.

His eyes caught mine, and there was heat there. Awareness. A flicker of surprise that matched mine—only he didn't bother hiding it.

"You expected me to be soft," he said, low and infuriatingly calm.

I jerked my hand back like I'd touched a live wire. "Don't flatter yourself. I didn't expect anything."

His mouth curved into that half-smile that made my stomach do something deeply inconvenient. "Liar."

"I'm not lying," I snapped, though the heat crawling up my neck said otherwise.

We were close now. Too close for oxygen. Too close for good decisions.

Close enough to smell his cologne—not overpowering, not trying too hard. Just... expensive. Clean. The kind of scent that whispered lean in closer and not in a creepy way.

Which was precisely what I was *not* going to do.

"You're infuriating," I muttered.

"The feeling's mutual," he murmured, voice rougher now.

And then—he stepped even closer.

I should've walked away.

I didn't.

"I've met a hundred women like you," he said, and the rasp in his voice betrayed him. "All thinking they've got me figured out."

"And I've met a dozen men like you," I fired back. "Born on third base, convinced they hit a triple."

His jaw flexed.

"You don't know anything about me."

"I know enough," I said—and the words hung there, hot and electric, full of fire and something else I didn't dare name.

My nipples tightened beneath my blouse, and a rush of heat pulsed between my legs—hot, aching, traitorous.

I should've hated this. I was supposed to hate this.

Instead, my body was lighting up like it hadn't gotten the memo.

"You want me to be the villain," he said, voice dropping to a near-growl. "Because that's easier."

I scoffed—wobbly. "And why wouldn't I? Guys like you make it so damn easy."

A muscle ticked in his jaw as he leaned in. Heat rolled off him like a warning.

"You want to know what I think?" he said, voice low and dangerous. "I think you're terrified I might *not* be the villain you need me to be."

His eyes dropped to my mouth, and something inside me short-circuited.

My breath caught. My skin flushed. Every inch of me suddenly aware of just how close he was.

Brett Wentworth was going to kiss me.

And the worst part?

Some unhinged, completely traitorous part of me wanted him to.

"Don't," I whispered, before that part of me got louder.

But it didn't come out strong. It came out like a dare.

He didn't move—just hovered there, close enough that I could feel the heat rolling off him. His voice dropped, low and dangerous.

"Don't what?"

"Don't kiss me," I said.

It was supposed to be a warning.

It sounded like a challenge.

That smirk again. Like he could see straight through me and was enjoying every second of it.

"Is that what you think I'm going to do?"

My cheeks flamed. "Isn't it?"

He leaned in—just a breath from my ear, voice low enough to melt reason.

"I don't kiss women who hate me."

A shiver shot down my spine, sharp and electric.

And then—he stepped back.

The air snapped between us like a pulled wire, leaving me breathless, buzzing, and completely unmoored.

"Have a good night, Ms. Bentley," he said, maddeningly even, already turning away like nothing had happened.

The sudden distance hit like whiplash. One second, he was all heat and temptation—close enough to undo me. The next? Gone.

Which was good.

Exactly what I wanted.

Exactly what I needed.

Right?

Then why did my body still ache like he'd taken something with him when he walked away?

Chapter Five

LIZ

I couldn't sleep that night. The ceiling of my bedroom had never been fascinating, but at 2:37 am, I'd memorized every crack and shadow. My mind replayed that moment in my office like a broken record—the heat in his eyes, the way his voice dropped, the intoxicating scent of his cologne. And the way he'd just... walked away. "Ugh!" I groaned, flipping onto my stomach and burying my face in my pillow. This was ridiculous. I didn't want Brett Wentworth to kiss me. I didn't want anything from him except professional distance and maybe, eventually, a glowing reference when I inevitably left for a company not run by an arrogant billionaire. So why couldn't I stop thinking about how his lips might have felt against mine? I reached for my phone, tempted to text Mia, but I knew exactly what she'd say. Something about "hate-kissing" and "sexual tension" that I absolutely did *not* need to hear right now.

I tossed my phone aside. This was insane. I sat up with a deep, weary sigh and ran my fingers through my tangled hair, feeling each knot and stray strand as if they were manifestations of my inner chaos. I chided myself; I was a grown, successful woman who had faced intimidating corporate execs, negotiated six-figure deals, and once told a department head that his marketing strategy was "embarrassingly outdated." I wasn't the type to melt over a maybe. But then again, I'd never stood that close to a man whose presence felt like a promise—and a threat—all in one.

"This is just chemistry," I muttered. "Annoying. Distracting. Temporary."

A blip. A glitch. The kind of thing easily resolved with a glass of wine, some denial, and a little help from the right toy.

Driven by a desperate need to regain control over my spiraling thoughts, I rolled over and yanked open the bedside drawer. Amidst a jumble of chargers, lip balms, and miscellaneous clutter, my fingers closed around the smooth, cool silicone of my trusted vibrator. It was a gift from Mia last Christmas—a playful, almost scandalous token wrapped in festive paper and accompanied by a card that cheekily read, "For when spreadsheets aren't enough excitement." I had laughed then, half-embarrassed and half-grateful, pushing it aside with a fleeting blush of amusement.

Now, holding it in my palm, it felt like a symbol of rationality—a simple, clinical outlet to channel my tangled arousal away from the mess that was Brett Wentworth. It was just a release. A reset. A way to clear the fog and get back to what really mattered.

The first touch made me gasp—I was already aching in a way that betrayed just how worked up I'd been.

"Damn him," I whispered, closing my eyes as I pressed the vibrator more firmly against my clit.

But closing my eyes was a mistake. Because suddenly, he was there—those dark eyes, that voice like honey and sin. I could feel the ghost of his breath at my ear, the imagined heat of his shoulders under my palms.

"This isn't about him," I reminded myself, but my body disagreed. The tension was building fast, embarrassingly fast, my hips rising to meet each pulse of the vibrator as I imagined what might have happened if I hadn't said "don't." If he had closed that final inch between us.

"Fuck," I gasped, my free hand clutching at the sheets as I came hard and sudden, waves of pleasure crashing through me with an intensity that left me trembling.

As the aftershocks faded, so did the temporary fog of satisfaction. I lay there, breathing hard, irritation bubbling up beneath the surface. Of all the fantasies to hijack my brain, it had to be him. Brett freaking Wentworth. The man I was determined to loathe. A distraction in a tailored suit whose presence was already too dangerous to ignore—professionally or otherwise.

"This never happened," I declared firmly to my quiet, empty room, as if convincing the silence could erase the memory. I cleaned it—because I'm not a complete degenerate—tossed it back in the drawer, and slammed it shut. Great. Now I could add *horny for the enemy* to my list of professional concerns.

***

I spent the entire morning rehearsing.

Every stat. Every rebuttal. Every slide.

Twenty-eight pages of indisputable proof that I was an asset Bright Spark couldn't afford to lose.

No heat. No tension. Just cool, corporate precision.

"You've got this," I muttered, collecting my laptop, notes, and client testimonials like armor. "He's just a man. A frustrating, smug, dangerously attractive—no. Just a man. Who signs your paychecks."

Each step toward Brett's office felt like a reset.

Click. I'm a professional.

Click. I am exceptional at my job.

Click. And any resemblance between last night's fantasy and my boss is purely coincidental.

His assistant glanced up as I approached. "He's expecting you, Ms. Bentley. Go on in."

Brett stood by the window when I walked in, sleeves rolled up, tie loosened, forearms casually ruining my focus.

Not helpful.

"Mr. Wentworth," I said crisply. "I've prepared a detailed overview of my portfolio and performance over the last three years."

I placed my laptop on the conference table, my movements precise and controlled. Ice queen, fully activated.

He turned, taking his time crossing the room. Then he leaned against the edge of his desk, arms crossed, watching me like he was waiting for me to blink.

"Thank you for being so thorough," he said, voice calm and infuriatingly deep. "But before we get to your presentation, there's something else we need to talk about."

I froze. "And what would that be?"

"We have a problem, Ms. Bentley."

My fingers tightened around my pen. "I wasn't aware of any issues with my performance."

He stepped forward, slow and deliberate. "This isn't about your performance."

Oh no.

"I don't know what you're talking about," I said—fast, unconvincing.

He kept coming. That subtle cologne hit my senses like a tranquilizer dart wrapped in lust.

"I think you do," he murmured. "There's something happening here. And it's getting harder to ignore."

"Mr. Wentworth—"

"Brett."

"I prefer Mr. Wentworth," I snapped, even as my voice wobbled. "And there is nothing between us."

His gaze swept over me. Calm. Too calm. "Then why can't you look me in the eye when you say that?"

I did. "I'm looking. And I'm telling you—we're strictly professional."

He stepped closer.

I backed up—straight into the conference table.

"Sure," he said, voice like velvet over steel. "That's why you're clutching that folder like it's a flotation device."

I glared. "You are wildly full of yourself."

"You were thinking about last night."

My breath caught.

Wait—what?

How the hell could he possibly know what I did last night?

He couldn't.

There's no way.

Unless he'd suddenly developed telepathy—or my vibrator had started sending status reports.

He tilted his head. "How I didn't kiss you."

Oh.

My stomach dropped—for a completely different reason.

Damn him.

"You're imagining things."

His lips curved. That maddening almost-smile. "Am I?"

He closed the distance, heat radiating off him like a furnace.

"Because I've been thinking about it too."

My pulse thundered in my throat.

"That's inappropriate, Mr. Wentworth."

"So is the way you're looking at me right now."

This was a nightmare.

A tall, broad-shouldered, unfairly attractive nightmare who smelled like bad choices and sin and made my brain short-circuit.

"I came here to discuss my job," I said tightly, gripping my folder like it might save me.

"And I came here to figure out why I can't stop thinking about you."

My mouth opened. Closed. Useless.

"Can we start the presentation?"

He smiled—slow, smug, and absolutely devastating.

"You're adorable when you're flustered."

"I'm not flustered."

"Keep telling yourself that."

His smile said he saw right through me.

And unfortunately, he wasn't wrong.

BRETT

She was flushed and breathless, her chest rising like she'd just run a mile. My presence was getting to her—and hell if that didn't light something dark and hungry in me.

"You want to hate me," I said, stepping close enough to feel her warmth. "It'd be a lot easier if you could."

"I do hate you," she snapped—too fast, too breathless.

That defiant gleam in her eyes? Still there. But now it was tangled with something else. Want. Sharp and raw and aimed straight at me.

"No," I murmured, inching closer. "You don't. And it's driving you crazy."

She didn't move. Didn't speak. She just stood there with her lips parted and her spine ramrod straight, as if her pride was the only thing holding her upright.

"Tell me to back off," I said low. "Tell me there's nothing here, and I'll step away. We'll go over your presentation like professionals. Like nothing happened."

She didn't.

Her eyes flicked to my mouth, and that was it. The last thread snapped.

I cupped her jaw gently, brushing my thumb along her cheekbone. "Last chance."

Her answer was a fistful of my shirt and a kiss that knocked the air from my lungs.

It was fire. It was the kind of kiss that stripped you bare—fast, fierce, and fucking inevitable.

She kissed like she fought—unyielding, intense, demanding. Our mouths clashed, tongues tangling, bodies colliding like we'd been circling this moment from the start.

I groaned into her mouth, dragging her closer. She gasped when I lifted her onto the table, and her legs wrapped around me instinctively. I pressed into her, letting her feel every hard inch of what she was doing to me.

"I hate you," she whispered against my lips, even as she arched into my touch.

"Sure you do," I growled, trailing my mouth along her neck.

My hands slid up her thighs, bunching her skirt. When I finally slipped my hand between her legs, I felt it—damp lace, hot aching need. And fuck if that didn't undo me.

"You're so fucking wet." I murmured, voice rough. "Tell me again how much you hate me."

She whimpered when I rubbed her through the fabric. Her fingers clenched my shoulders, nails digging in.

"I—loathe you," she panted, hips grinding down against my hand.

I chuckled against her throat. "That so?"

She tugged my hair—hard. "Don't stop."

That was all I needed.

I pushed her panties aside, sliding one finger into her slick heat. She clenched around me, tight and perfect. Her lips parted in a breathy moan that went straight to my cock.

"Fuck," I muttered. "You feel incredible."

"Brett." My name came out like a plea.

I added a second finger, my thumb circling her clit. Her body rocked against me, breath hitching, eyes fluttering shut.

"That's it," I whispered. "Come for me, Elizabeth. Show me how much you don't want this."

She trembled, head thrown back, muscles tightening. I watched it hit her—the way she shattered, silently at first, then with a gasp that would haunt my dreams. Her body pulsed around my fingers, her thighs trembling.

I kissed her hard as she came, swallowing the moan that ripped out of her. When she slumped against me, dazed and wrecked, I slowly pulled my fingers free, watching her reaction.

Her gaze was heavy-lidded. Lips kiss-swollen. Hair slipping from her ponytail.

I brought my fingers to my lips and sucked them clean—slow, deliberate, never breaking eye contact.

She stared, jaw slack.

"Jesus," she whispered.

"You taste even better than I imagined," I said softly.

A knock shattered the moment.

"Mr. Wentworth?" my assistant called through the door. "Your two o'clock is here early."

I froze.

Another knock.

"Just a moment," I called, fighting to steady my breathing.

Elizabeth was already moving, pulling her skirt down, smoothing her blouse, and brushing trembling fingers through her hair. She wouldn't look at me.

I tucked in my shirt and straightened my tie, though my body was still coiled with want.

"We're not done," I said, stepping toward her.

Her eyes flew to mine, wide and burning. "Yes, we are. This—" her voice cracked, "was a mistake."

I flinched.

"Elizabeth, wait. We'll talk after—"

"There's nothing to say," she bit out. "It meant nothing."

"Liz—"

"Don't call me that," she said, voice low and sharp. "You don't get to call me that."

And then she was gone.

The door clicked shut behind her, leaving behind the echo of her voice, the heat of her body, and the storm we'd just unleashed—raw, reckless, impossible to ignore.

Chapter Six

LIZ

I STORMED PAST BRETT'S assistant like a woman possessed, ignoring the poor guy in reception who blinked at me like I might explode. Honestly, he wasn't wrong to be scared.

I stabbed the elevator button like it owed me money. When the doors opened, I practically dove inside and collapsed against the wall, heart pounding. The second they slid shut, I let out a sound that was half-wheeze, half-deranged laugh.

Oh. My. God.

I had just— He had just— We had just—

"Shit. Shit. Shit."

My underwear was still damp. My pulse was still thudding. And the man responsible?

Brett freaking Wentworth.

The man I was supposed to hate.

The man who signs my paychecks.

The man who now knew *exactly* what I sounded like mid-orgasm.

Amazing. Love that for me.

Downstairs, the receptionist gave me a once-over that clearly said: *damn, girl*—like she couldn't decide whether to call security or offer me a glass of water.

I didn't stop. I shot out the building like daylight might somehow scorch the memory off my skin.

Spoiler: it didn't.

By the time I got home, I looked like I'd barely survived a rave. Ponytail half-collapsed, lipstick smudged, blouse askew—like I'd stumbled through a battlefield instead of a boardroom.

I slammed the door behind me and kicked off my heels with enough force to launch one under the couch. Good. Let it live there.

"What the hell were you thinking?" I hissed at my reflection.

The woman staring back at me? She didn't look like Elizabeth Bentley: competent, capable, senior account executive.

She looked like someone who'd just short-circuited her entire life for a man with great bone structure and hands that could ruin empires.

I yanked off my jacket like it had betrayed me and stomped into the bedroom, stripping as I went.

The blouse? Gone.

The skirt? Dead to me.

The lace underwear? Gone. Tossed into the hamper like it personally betrayed me.

I caught sight of myself again in the mirror. Flushed. Damp. Eyes blown wide with leftover lust.

"Pull it together," I muttered, stomping into the bathroom and cranking the shower like I wanted to steam-clean my brain.

The water scalded. Didn't help.

I scrubbed until my skin turned pink and my heart finally slowed. But the echo of his voice still hummed in my ear. The ghost of his mouth still tingled on mine. And between my thighs? A memory I couldn't shake.

Wrapped in the biggest towel I owned, I collapsed onto the edge of the bed.

My phone buzzed.

Of course it did.

Mia:

Where did you go???

*Diana from accounting said you **ran**.*

Are you okay???

Elizabeth Bentley, I swear to God, if you don't answer me, I'm coming over.

With wine.

And snacks.

And QUESTIONS.

I groaned and hit call. She picked up on the first ring.

"Oh THANK GOD, she *lives*," Mia said. "I was about to file a missing persons report and list your last known location as 'inside your own corporate shame spiral'."

"I'm fine," I lied. Badly.

"Try again."

"I got a migraine."

"Bullshit. You get stress headaches and power through them like a demon in heels."

"Mia—"

"Wait." A beat. "Did he fire you?"

I let out a too-loud, slightly manic laugh. "No. He... *definitely* didn't fire me."

"Elizabeth Marie Bentley," she said, voice deadly serious. "What happened?"

"Nothing."

"Oh. My. God. You hooked up with him."

"No."

"You *so* did! Was it a kissing moment? A desk moment? A public-indecency-and-an-HR-lawsuit moment?"

I flopped back onto the bed with a groan. "It was one moment. A heat-of-the-moment, hormones-hijacked-my-brain moment."

Mia gasped so loud I had to yank the phone away from my ear.

"You did the deed in his office, didn't you?"

"No one did any deed!"

"Then what *did* happen?"

"We kissed. There may have been fingers involved. It was... a very poor choice."

There was a pause. Then:

"Tell me everything. Right now. Or I swear I'll haunt your ass forever."

"I'm never going back to the office again."

"Yes, you are. And when you do, I want you looking like the patron saint of bad decisions—with a killer strut and absolutely no regrets."

I sighed. "I hate you."

"No you don't. But you *do* have it bad."

I hung up before she could say *hot and bothered* again.

Then I lay there, towel slipping, chest heaving, heart pounding.

What the hell had I done?

And worse—

Why did part of me want to do it again?

BRETT

I left the office after my two o'clock meeting.

Not because the day was done—far from it—but because I couldn't sit in that building one second longer without thinking about what had happened in my damn office.

I didn't say anything to my assistant on the way out. Just grabbed my jacket, shut the door behind me, and headed straight to the elevator like I had someplace important to be.

My car was waiting out front.

My driver raised an eyebrow when I slid into the backseat—it wasn't exactly quitting time—but he didn't comment. Just pulled away from the curb like we did this every day.

'Home, sir?' he asked after a beat

"Yeah," I said quietly. "Home."

I wasn't heading home to relax or clear my schedule. I just needed space—from the woman who'd short-circuited every logical thought I'd had since walking into Bright Spark.

I stared out the window, jaw tight, fists clenched in my lap.

I almost told him to take a detour. Just a quick stop. Just to check on her.

But I didn't.

Because I knew if I saw her again tonight, I wouldn't be able to keep my hands off her. Wouldn't be able to think straight. Wouldn't stop at just touching her. I would tear her fucking clothes off and bury myself so deeply in that hot tight pussy that I wouldn't know where I ended, and she began.

The car rolled to a stop in front of my building. I stepped out without a word, and the doorman greeted me as I crossed the marble lobby.

"Good evening, Mr. Wentworth."

I managed a curt nod in response, already jabbing the elevator button. The doors slid open immediately as if sensing my urgency. My reflection stared back from the mirrored walls—flushed face, disheveled hair, eyes dark with barely contained need.

I looked like a man on the edge.

The elevator ascended to the penthouse, and I was grateful for the privacy. My cock had been painfully hard since the moment her lips touched mine, and the pressure of my slacks was becoming unbearable. Her taste was still on my tongue, her scent on my fingers, and I could hear the little gasp she'd made when I'd slid my fingers inside her.

"Fuck," I growled, tossing my keys onto the marble counter with enough force to send them skidding across the surface.

I needed a drink. A cold shower. A lobotomy. Anything to get Elizabeth Bentley out of my head.

I poured three fingers of whiskey, not bothering with ice, and downed half of it in one burning swallow. The alcohol hit my system but did nothing to cool the heat raging through me. If anything, it just loosened what little restraint I had left.

I stalked to the floor-to-ceiling windows that overlooked the city. The sun was setting, painting it in shades of gold and amber. Somewhere out there, Elizabeth was probably cursing my name, trying to convince herself that what happened was a mistake.

But it wasn't. It was fucking inevitable. She just hadn't accepted it yet.

I drained the rest of my whiskey, feeling it burn all the way down. Setting the glass on the side table with more force than necessary, I unbuttoned my shirt, suddenly feeling confined. Constrained. Like my own fucking skin was too tight.

The memory of her taste lingered on my tongue—sweet, tangy, addictive. I wanted more. A lot more. And that terrified me.

I wasn't used to wanting something I couldn't have. Wasn't used to this gnawing, insistent ache that wouldn't subside no matter how much I tried to ignore it.

I stripped off my shirt and headed for the shower, turning the water as cold as possible. The icy spray hit my overheated skin like needles, but it did nothing to cool the fire burning inside me. If anything, the sensation just heightened everything—every nerve ending, every memory of her body against mine.

"Goddammit," I muttered, bracing one hand against the tile wall.

I gave in to the inevitable, wrapping my hand around my aching cock. The first stroke sent a jolt of pleasure so intense it bordered on pain. I closed my eyes, and she was there—those blue eyes challenging me, that mouth parted in a silent gasp, those fingers digging into my shoulders as she came undone.

I stroked harder, faster, imagining what it would have been like if we hadn't been interrupted. If I'd spread her thighs and buried myself deep inside her. The sounds she would have made. The way she would have felt, hot and tight around my cock.

"Elizabeth," I groaned, the sound echoing off the shower walls as I came hard, spilling over my hand. The release was intense but hollow—a poor substitute for what I really wanted.

I stayed under the cold spray for several minutes, trying to regain some semblance of control. But I knew it was pointless. Something fundamental had shifted today, and there was no going back.

Chapter Seven

BRETT

When Mia cornered me in the elevator the next morning and said, "You're coming to the prototype floor," I thought she was joking.

She wasn't.

"Investor tour's tomorrow," she added, already texting someone—possibly Satan. "You can't pitch what you haven't experienced. Liz is setting up the Adventure Kit now."

Of course she was.

Because nothing screams *let's pretend our wildly inappropriate office hookup never happened* like foam swords and suction-cup arrows.

I stepped into the prototype room, and there she was.

Liz.

Bent over a crate of gear, blonde curls pulled back, blouse tucked into a pencil skirt that should not have been legal this early in the morning.

She looked up.

Our eyes locked for one loaded, breathless second.

Then she blinked—armor slamming into place.

Chin up. Mouth tight. Sarcasm cocked and ready.

"Let me guess," she said, tone cool enough to chill concrete. "Mia threatened you."

"She's terrifying," Liz muttered, yanking a foam sword from a crate like she wanted to stab something. Possibly me. "But she's not wrong. Investors eat this stuff up."

The air between us was charged—every breath thick with the memory of last night. Her legs wrapped around me. Her moan in my ear. The way she'd whispered my name like a secret.

I cleared my throat. "So. Where do you want me?"

She hesitated.

Not long. Not noticeably. But enough.

Enough to know I wasn't the only one remembering.

Then, without looking at me, she nodded toward the far end of the setup. "Start at the tunnel. Try not to sprain anything."

There it was—dismissive, efficient, and just sharp enough to cut.

I deserved it.

But fuck if it didn't make me want her all over again.

I looked around the obstacle course like it was a war zone. Foam tunnels. Rope coils. A warning sign that read *LAVA PIT: DO NOT CROSS*.

"This is for the demo?"

"Yep." Liz knelt beside a bin of suction darts, her ponytail swaying as she pulled out gear. "Build-Your-Own Quest Kit. Ages six to ten. Obstacle pieces, costumes, a mission scroll, and enough ways to humiliate yourself to last a lifetime." She stood and tossed me a rope coil like it was a grenade. "You'll fit right in."

"I don't play," I said flatly.

She smiled sweetly. "You're about to. Use your imagination. Builds character."

Ten minutes later, I was tangled in netting, wedged halfway through a foam tunnel that was definitely not built for a six-foot-four adult male.

Leaning casually against the wall, Liz crossed her arms, biting back a grin.

"You look comfy," she said.

"This is a trap."

"You're just mad a ten-year-old would've beat your time."

"I'm six-foot-four."

"All that height and no coordination. It's tragic, really."

I finally crawled out, pride limping behind me. Foam bits clung to my pants. My shirt was untucked. My dignity was on life support.

"You're enjoying this," I muttered.

Liz didn't even try to deny it. "Watching you get outsmarted by a children's obstacle course? Highlight of my week."

Her eyes sparkled—real this time, unguarded. And when our eyes met, the moment stretched. A flicker of something passed between us, something warm and dangerous, like we were both remembering and pretending not to.

Then she turned, already reaching for the next setup.

"Come on, Wentworth," she called over her shoulder. "Let's see if you can survive the suction dart gauntlet."

"How'd you come up with this?" I asked.

She blinked, instantly more guarded. "What?"

"This kit. Mia said it was yours."

Her posture tightened for a beat—then she lifted her chin. "We brainstormed the idea together. But the layout? The mechanics? That's me."

I nodded. "It's smart. Really smart. And fun. Engaging. It's kind of... brilliant."

Her lips parted like she wanted to argue. Then shut again.

"It makes sense now," I said. "Why you fight so hard for this place."

She hesitated, the shield not quite back up. "It matters. To a lot of people."

I nodded. "Yeah. I'm starting to get that."

Then she tilted her head. "What about you?"

"What about me?"

"Why are you really here?" she asked. Not accusing. Just... curious.

"You could've walked away," she said. "Sold the company. Let someone else clean up the mess. But you didn't."

I looked at her. Really looked at her. And gave her the truth.

"I was running my own company," I said. "Logistics—warehousing, supply chain, the boring stuff that keeps the world spinning. I built it from nothing. Scaled it. Sold it for a number that still feels fake."

She didn't blink.

"I didn't use my dad's name. Didn't take a cent from him. I was tired of people thinking I was just coasting on someone else's legacy."

A flicker of something crossed her face. Her spine stayed straight, her jaw firm—but her cheeks flushed, just slightly.

She had the grace not to look away.

I paused. Then: "And then my dad called."

Her posture shifted. Just slightly.

"He told me Bright Spark was drowning. Contracts tanking. Clients bailing. Half the staff gone. And he hadn't even noticed—until it was almost too late."

I looked down at the foam sword in my hands.

"I could've let it fall. But I couldn't stop thinking about what it was supposed to be."

I turned the sword slowly in my fingers.

"When I was a kid, all I wanted was for my dad to pay attention, to play with me. Not big things. Just time. Focus. Not a tablet and a distracted 'go play.' But something real."

I looked at her again.

"That's what Bright Spark was supposed to be. A way for kids to imagine. Connect. Be seen. I didn't have that. But I could help make sure other kids did."

"You're not what I expected," she said softly.

I met her gaze. "Neither are you."

LIZ

I wasn't ready for that.

Not the story.

Not the quiet way he told it.

Not the gut-punch realization that I'd had him all wrong.

I'd painted Brett Wentworth in bold, unapologetic strokes: entitled, arrogant, probably had a yacht named after his golden retriever.

But this?

He hadn't coasted. He'd clawed his way to success, built something real, and stayed when he could've walked away from his father's mess.

And dammit, that did something to me.

Something warm and terrifying and way too inconvenient.

I looked away, mostly so he couldn't see the expression flickering across my face—whatever it was. But he didn't press.

He just stood there. Still. Steady. Present.

Which somehow made it worse.

"I used to think," I said before I could stop myself, "that if I just worked hard enough, no one could take anything from me."

He turned slightly toward me. Listening.

"I was the girl with the color-coded planner. Honor student. Every scholarship form submitted six weeks early." I let out a laugh that felt hollow. "None of it mattered."

I paused. Took a breath. The kind that felt like bracing for impact.

"There was this guy in college. Bradley." I didn't bother hiding the bitterness in my voice. "I thought he cared about me. I thought we were something real. But I was wrong. He used me. Copied my work—word for word. He got caught... and blamed me."

I swallowed.

"He had a last name that opened doors. A dad with deep pockets. I had a partial scholarship and an academic advisor who barely remembered my name."

I looked down at my hands. "He graduated. I didn't. One class short."

The silence stretched again.

"I never told anyone," I added, voice quieter now. "Not even my mom. I just... rewrote the story."

And now, it was out there.

Raw.

True.

I glanced at Brett.

No pity. No judgment.

Just... understanding.

And somehow, that was worse than pity.

Because suddenly, I didn't feel like I was staring at the enemy.

I felt like I was standing across from someone who knew exactly what it meant to be underestimated.

He leaned in, just enough to make my breath hitch.

His hand lifted—hesitating in the space between us.

Like he didn't know if he should touch me.

And God help me, I wanted him to.

But before he could—

"Hey!" Mia's voice rang from the hallway. "How's it going in—oh."

She stepped inside, blinked once, then smiled like she knew a secret we didn't.

"Well. No one's bleeding. That's a win."

I jerked back like we'd been caught making out behind the gym. "We were just wrapping up."

Mia glanced between us, eyes dancing. All sunshine and chaos. "Uh-huh. Well, I need you to look at the new prototypes before I throw my laptop, and myself, out the nearest window. You good here, Brett?"

He nodded once. Cool. Controlled. Already rebuilding whatever wall I'd watched crack just moments ago.

I nodded too—too fast. "Right. Yes. Prototypes. Absolutely."

Mia arched an eyebrow but didn't say anything. Just bumped me with her elbow, like she hadn't just interrupted a moment with a capital M, and turned for the hallway.

I followed, pulse still skittering.

And I didn't look back.

Because I wasn't entirely sure I'd be able to walk away if I did.

Chapter Eight

BRETT

Investor tours were always a performance.

Polished smiles. Polite nods. Just enough innovation to dazzle, just enough stability to soothe.

But today?

Today felt different.

Maybe because the stakes were higher.

Maybe because the company's future was riding on this.

Or maybe because every time I looked across the room and saw Liz—confident, poised, utterly magnetic—something inside me shifted.

She led a group of investors through the Adventure Kit demo, explaining how the obstacle components promoted movement, problem-solving, and teamwork. Her voice was clear and warm.

"She's good," Mia said beside me, not even pretending to be casual.

"I know," I said.

And I did. God, I did.

She was everything this company was supposed to be—clever, innovative, fearless. Watching her command the room felt like watching the future unfold in real time.

I barely had time to let that thought settle when the elevator dinged.

And everything inside me went still.

William Wentworth II.

Custom suit. Power tie. That arrogant glint in his eye like he'd just walked into *his* empire.

"What the hell is he doing here?" Mia muttered.

"No clue," I said, already bracing.

The air shifted the second he stepped out. Conversations stalled. Postures straightened. Most of the investors recognized him instantly.

My father smiled like a man who still thought the room belonged to him.

"Good morning! What an incredible showing. Wonderful to see such excitement about Bright Spark's future."

Liz paused mid-sentence. Turned.

Found me across the room.

Her eyes narrowed—confused. Guarded. A silent, *What is happening?*

I started toward her. One step. Two.

And then my father kept talking.

"I just want to say how proud I am of the leadership here," he said, voice booming. "Especially my son, Brett."

No.

"This," he gestured to the setup, "is exactly the kind of creativity I envisioned when I stepped aside."

No. No. **NO**.

"I was blown away," he went on, "when Brett brought me the Adventure Kit. He said, 'Let's give kids a way to imagine again. Let's get them moving.' And I thought—this, *this* is leadership!"

Polite applause followed. Tepid. Obligatory.

But I didn't hear any of it.

Because the moment William started talking, Liz had gone quiet.

Mid-sentence, mid-presentation—just... stopped.

Now she stood frozen across the room, still and silent.

Her gaze cut to my father.

Then to me.

And I saw the exact second her expression changed.

Not to anger. Not even to hurt.

To something worse.

Resignation.

The kind that said, *of course.* Like she'd been foolish to believe it could ever end any other way.

She walked away and didn't look back—and somehow, that hurt more than if she'd told me off.

Mia who had been filming the investor preview, appeared at my elbow.

Her voice was low, cold. "Fix it."

So I did the only thing I could.

I stepped forward.

"Thank you, William," I said into the quiet. My voice was sharp. Flat. Hard.

The room turned to me. My father stilled.

"But, there's been a mistake."

A few eyebrows lifted.

"The Adventure Kit wasn't my idea. I didn't pitch it. I didn't design it. I didn't bring it to life."

A wave of confused murmurs rippled through the group.

"It was Elizabeth Bentley."

My father's jaw tightened.

"She and Mia Wilder co-developed the concept," I said. "Liz designed the structure, the framework, the mission system. Every interactive element you saw today? That was her."

Silence.

Wide eyes.

A few startled blinks.

"And I'm not going to take credit for her brilliance."

My father opened his mouth—probably to spin it—but I didn't let him.

"If you're impressed by today," I told the investors, "then you're impressed with her."

I turned on my heel and headed for the door.

I didn't know where she'd gone.

But I wasn't letting her walk away. Not like this.

LIZ

The elevator doors slid shut behind me, but William Wentworth's voice still echoed in my ears.

Brett's idea.

Brett's pitch.

Brett's execution.

I didn't wait. Just walked—out of the elevator, down the hall, through the lobby—past the receptionist without so much as a glance.

Under the Bright Spark logo I used to be proud to walk beneath.

My vision blurred, but I didn't cry. Not here.

I just kept moving. Out into the spring air that felt too bright, too sharp—like the world hadn't gotten the memo that everything had just cracked apart.

Half a block later, I dropped onto a bench facing the park. Breathing like it required effort. Like my body had to manually remind itself how.

And then it hit me. Nausea, swift and brutal. Not just from the adrenaline crash, but from the truth settling in my gut.

He let it happen.

Brett.

He stood there and let his father rewrite my work into *his* legacy.

The same man who told me I mattered.

Who crawled through foam tunnels just to make me laugh.

Who opened up about his childhood and wanting something real.

And because he let me in—I let him in, too.

I told him about Bradley. About the sleepless nights and the stolen future.

Because his family had legacy status and lawyers on speed dial—and mine had work-study and scholarships.

I told Brett everything.

And I really thought—maybe this time would be different.

But it wasn't.

He stayed silent.

And something in me broke.

The hope I'd been holding onto cracked apart in that quiet.

I don't know how long I sat there.

Just long enough for the adrenaline to drain, for the humiliation to settle in, and for the awful truth to sink deep—

I let him matter.

And now I wished I hadn't.

Then—

"Liz."

I didn't turn.

He approached slowly, like I might spook and bolt.

Smart of him.

"Please," he said softly. "Let me explain."

I laughed.

Brittle. Cold. The kind of laugh that kept heartbreak from slipping through.

"Sure. Go ahead. Spin your version. Make it sound noble."

He flinched.

Good.

"Liz, I didn't know he was going to say that." His voice was rough. Unsteady. "I didn't even know he was going to be there. I never told him the Adventure Kit was my idea. I haven't even spoken to him in weeks. You have to believe me."

I turned to face him, every nerve ending flaring like a warning light. "You stood there while he handed you credit for something *I* built. And you said *nothing*."

"I did," he said quickly. "After you walked out—"

"Too late." My voice wavered, but I held the line.

He looked gutted.

And maybe he had tried.

But the damage was done.

"I told you about Bradley." The words came out soft—barely more than a breath. "I told you what it felt like to be erased. And you let it happen again."

His jaw tensed. "It wasn't the same—"

"It was exactly the same."

That landed.

Sharp and clean and cruel.

"You knew what that moment meant," I said. "You knew. And you still stood there."

I stepped past him.

No hesitation.

No glance back.

Because for the first time since he walked into my life, I saw him for who he really was.

And I wasn't about to let *Billy* Wentworth be the one who broke me.

Chapter Nine

BRETT

I DIDN'T GO AFTER her.

By the time I got my feet to move, she was already down the block.

She didn't look back.

She didn't have to.

I'd already seen it on her face—not anger, but something heavier.

Disappointment.

Like she'd expected better... and realized too late that I wasn't it.

And honestly? I couldn't blame her.

She'd trusted me—with the kind of truth you don't hand out unless you think someone's different. Safer. Worth the risk.

And then my father stood there and took credit for her work, and I stayed silent.

Not forever.

Just long enough to feel like betrayal.

She told me what it cost her last time. What it felt like to be erased. And I let her think I'd done the same thing.

I pulled out my phone. Stared at it.

Then hit call.

Logan picked up on the first ring.

"Please tell me you're free to get a drink."

"Define *free*," he said.

There was a pause. A shuffle. Then, a shift in tone:

"Yes, ma'am, one mojito coming right up."

I blinked. "What the fuck—?"

"Hang on, sunshine, gotta fetch more limes."

"Logan." I said it like a threat.

"I'm at one of the resorts," he said, way too casually. "Site visit. Got mistaken for staff."

I snorted. "That's what you get for wearing those stupid Hawaiian shirts and flip-flops instead of dressing like a respectable CEO."

"I am *deeply* respected," he said. "Especially by the red-head who now thinks I coordinate guest experiences and lead sunset hikes."

"You're a menace."

"I'm thriving."

I exhaled hard, dragging a hand down my face. "I'm losing my damn mind."

"Okay. No jokes for a second—what happened?"

I didn't say anything—but apparently, I didn't need to. Logan's tone softened.

"This about her?"

"She walked out. Didn't look back."

"...Shit."

"Yeah."

"You want me to come back?"

"No. You've got beach chairs to alphabetize."

"She also thinks I lead paddleboard yoga at sunrise. Naturally, I've committed."

"You should be committed. Preferably somewhere with padded walls and no Wi-Fi. I hope she writes a scathing review."

"She's writing a *feature*," Logan said proudly. "And if it doesn't include the phrase *'charmingly rogue guest coordinator'*, I'll be devastated."

I groaned. "You're the reason warning labels exist."

"And you're spiraling," he said. "Go fix it."

LIZ

The spoon scraped the bottom of the pint with a sad little rustle—like even the ice cream was judging me.

I stared down at the empty container in my lap.

Contemplated the freezer.

Pint number two—chocolate fudge brownie—was in there. Tempting me with the kind of sweet nothings that always end in regret.

I didn't move.

Instead, I sighed and sank deeper into the couch cushions like a human burrito of regret.

My phone buzzed.

Again.

Another text from Mia. Number eight, if you were counting. (I was.)

Buzz. Nine.

Buzz. Ten.

I groaned. "Mia, if this is another cat meme, I swear—"

I flipped the phone over.

MIA:

You're going to regret ignoring me.

You need to watch this.

Seriously, Liz. Just watch it.

A video file waited beneath her text.

My thumb hovered.

Then tapped.

The screen lit up: the investor floor. The place where everything went to hell.

My stomach clenched, but I kept watching.

William Wentworth was mid-speech, soaking up credit he hadn't earned.

My fists clenched.

But then—

"There's been a mistake," Brett said.

My head snapped up.

"The Adventure Kit wasn't my idea I didn't pitch it. I didn't design it. I didn't bring it to life. That was Elizabeth Bentley."

Wait—what?

The camera was angled toward the front, but behind Brett, I caught it.

A flash of movement.

Me.

Still in the room.

He'd started speaking—*before* I walked out.

I just hadn't heard him.

Because I hadn't let myself.

I'd been so caught in the past—betrayal, heartbreak, and *Bradley*—that I never even gave Brett a chance to be anything else.

But he told the truth.

Right there. In front of investors. In front of his father.

"If you're impressed today, then you're impressed with her."

He looked wrecked in the video. Not smug. Not polished.

And I had walked out.

Not because he failed me.

Because I didn't wait long enough to see him *not* fail.

I set the phone down, heart pounding, throat tight.

God, I'd been so sure. I was so absolutely certain I knew what had happened. And I was wrong.

Brett hadn't taken anything.

He'd tried to fix it.

He'd defended me when it mattered.

And I'd missed it.

I swiped at my eyes. Stood up.

There was only one place I needed to be.

One man I needed to see.

I just hoped I wasn't already too late.

***

I'd never been to Brett's building before.

I'd seen it, sure—sleek, quiet-rich, high-rise energy. Black stone. Gold trim. The doorman with a Bluetooth earpiece that probably ran diagnostics on satellites.

Inside, it looked like a museum, and a Scandinavian furniture store had a baby and raised it on prestige TV.

My flip flops squeaked on the marble as I crossed the lobby. The doorman looked up—sixties, polished, with the kind of raised eyebrow that could shatter your self-esteem.

"Can I help you, miss?"

"Hi. Yes. I'm here to see Brett Wentworth."

I sounded calm. Composed.

Like I hadn't just cried into a hoodie and demolished a pint of salted caramel ice cream with a soup spoon.

He scanned me—frizzy hair, smudged sweatshirt, tote bag half-falling off my shoulder.

His expression didn't shift, but the *judgment* radiated off him like fine cologne.

"I'm afraid Mr. Wentworth has no appointments listed this evening."

"I know. I mean—I don't have an appointment, but he knows me. Liz Bentley. We work together." My voice lifted slightly at the end, hopeful.

He blinked once. The kind of blink that said *Oh, honey. No.*

"Yes," I said firmly. "He does know me. Really."

A pause.

Then he gave a polite, practiced smile that somehow managed to say *You poor, delusional thing.*

"I'm afraid I can't let anyone up without prior authorization."

"Can't you just... call him?"

"I'm afraid I'm not at liberty—"

"Please." My voice cracked. "It's important."

He hesitated. Then reached for the phone.

"Name?"

"Liz Bentley." I repeated.

He nodded. Pressed a button. "Sir, I have a Ms. Bentley here asking to see you... Yes... Understood."

He hung up. Straightened his jacket.

"Mr. Wentworth said to send you up."

I exhaled.

"Elevator's on your right. Top floor." Then, with a faint smile, "And miss?"

I turned.

"You might want to fix your hair. Just a bit."

I blinked. "Right. Thanks."

I stepped into the elevator, nerves on fire.

And prayed I wasn't too late.

CHAPTER TEN

BRETT

I HAD JUST POURED myself a drink I didn't need—bourbon, with a splash of guilt—when the phone buzzed.

"Sir, I have a Ms. Bentley here asking to see you."

I froze.

Liz. Here.

After everything.

"Send her up," I said before I could overthink it.

I didn't know what she was going to say. Hell, I didn't even know what *I* was going to say. But I knew one thing for sure:

I wasn't letting her walk away again.

The private elevator chimed.

I turned.

And there she was.

Hair a little windblown, hoodie zipped halfway up, tote bag sliding off her shoulder like it was clinging to her out of pure desperation. She looked unsure.

And completely beautiful.

Then she drew in a breath and stepped out.

"I saw the video," she said, voice quiet but steady.

My pulse kicked up. "What video?"

"Mia filmed the investor pitch." A humorless laugh escaped her. "Caught the whole thing—including you. Telling the truth. Giving me credit."

I blinked. "You watched it?"

She nodded. "Saw myself walk out right as you started talking. I didn't hear a word of it. I was so sure..." She trailed off, the disbelief still there. "I thought I knew exactly what happened."

I stepped closer, slow and careful. "You were hurting. I get it."

She gave me a look. "I said some pretty awful things."

I shrugged. "Please. You've called me worse—this week."

Her lips twitched, and for a second, I let myself hope.

We just stood there. No walls. No armor. Just everything unsaid hanging between us.

Then, she took another step forward.

"I was wrong," she said. "I should've stayed. I should've trusted you."

I shook my head. "You had every reason not to."

"Brett—"

"No, let me finish," I said gently. "What my father pulled today... I get why it hit the way it did. Some wounds don't heal all the way."

She nodded once.

"I had you pegged from day one," she said. "Trust fund guy. Polished. Entitled. I judged you before I even knew you."

"And now?"

"Now..." She met my eyes, honest and wide open. "I don't know. That's why I'm here."

My heart thudded. I closed the distance between us.

"Ask me," I said. "Anything."

She looked at me for a long beat. "Why did you really come to Bright Spark?"

"I told you before—it wasn't about saving my father's legacy. It was about the company. What it stood for." I paused. "But now? Now there's more."

"More?" she echoed, voice barely above a whisper.

"You." I stepped in closer.

"I've spent my whole life trying to prove I'm more than just a name. Then you walked into my office—sharp, stubborn—and saw exactly what everyone else sees."

She winced. "I did."

"I don't blame you. You weren't entirely wrong. I was born into privilege. A name. A legacy. But I built something of my own—no shortcuts, no handouts. And when my dad called about Bright Spark, I almost stayed away."

I paused.

"But I didn't. I showed up. And then I met you."

Her eyes softened.

"And suddenly, none of it was about legacy or redemption. It was about showing up for the things that matter. The ideas that matter. The people who matter. For you."

A long beat passed.

"You stood up for me," she said.

"I should've done it sooner."

"You did it when it mattered. When everyone who needed to hear it was listening."

"But you didn't hear it," I said quietly. "That's what kills me."

"I'm hearing it now," she whispered.

She stepped closer. So close I could feel the heat between us.

Then she reached up and touched my jaw—fingertips light like she wasn't sure I was real.

"I came here tonight because I needed to know," she said. "If what I saw in that video… was real."

I covered her hand with mine, pressing it to my cheek. "I'm real, Liz. What I feel for you is real."

Her eyes locked on mine. "And what do you feel?"

"Like you walked in, turned everything upside down, and somehow made it make more sense.

Her lips parted. Her breath caught.

"You walked in that first day like you were ready to set the building on fire," I said. "You've been under my skin ever since. You're brilliant. Relentless. Honest to a fault. And yeah, you make me crazy. But I want you. All of you. Not just the fire. I want the heart. The trust. The future."

She stared at me, eyes wide. "I don't do halfway, Brett."

"I'm not asking for halfway." I stepped even closer, our bodies nearly touching now. "I'm asking for everything."

The silence stretched. Not heavy. Not scary. Just full.

Then she smiled—small but sure.

"I want everything, too," she said.

And just like that—every breath I'd been holding released in one dizzying rush.

I cupped her face, brushing my thumb over her cheek. She leaned into the touch like she'd been waiting for it forever.

And maybe she had.

Because I knew I had.

"You sure?" I whispered.

"Ask me again after you kiss me," she whispered, a wicked little spark in her eyes.

LIZ

I breathed in, feeling my heart hammering against my ribs as Brett's eyes lingered on mine. The air between us crackled with electricity, with every confession and admission still hovering in the space we shared. He leaned in slowly, his hand sliding to the back of my neck, fingers tangling in my hair.

"Liz," he whispered, my name a prayer on his lips.

And then his mouth was on mine.

Not like before—frantic and desperate in his office. This was different. Deeper. Slower. Like he was memorizing me. His lips moved against mine with a tenderness that made my knees weak, a stark contrast to the heat building between us.

I melted into him, my hands sliding up his chest to grip his shoulders. He tasted like bourbon and promise—warm, rich, intoxicating. My tote bag slid from my shoulder, landing on the floor with a soft thud, but neither of us cared. Nothing mattered except this moment, this connection that felt like coming home after being lost for too long.

His arms wrapped around my waist, pulling me closer until there wasn't a breath of space between us. I gasped against his mouth as his tongue swept across my lower lip, seeking entrance. I opened to him without hesitation, my body arching into his as the kiss deepened.

When we finally broke apart, both breathing hard, his forehead rested against mine. His eyes were darker now, pupils blown wide with desire, but there was something else there too—vulnerability, honesty, raw emotion that made my chest ache.

"I've been thinking about you," he murmured, his voice rough and low. "Every day. Every night. Since that moment in my office."

My pulse quickened. "Have you?"

"Every minute," he confessed, his voice dropping to that delicious low register that made warmth pool in my belly. "I can't get you out of my head, Liz. The way you felt under my hands, the sounds you made, the taste of you—it's been driving me crazy."

The raw honesty in his admission sent a shiver down my spine. His hands slid to my waist, thumbs brushing against the sliver of skin where my hoodie had ridden up. Even that simple touch felt electric.

"I've been lying awake at night," he continued, "thinking about what would have happened if we hadn't been interrupted. Imagining all the ways I want to touch you, taste you."

I swallowed hard, my body responding to his words as intensely as his touch. The heat between us was building, transforming into something urgent and primal.

"Show me," I whispered, surprising myself with my boldness.

His eyebrows lifted slightly. "Show you what?"

I stepped back just enough to look at him fully, my heart pounding wildly against my ribs. The words formed on my lips before I could second-guess them.

"Show me what you do when you think about me," I said, my voice steadier than I felt. "When you're alone. I want to see what I've been missing."

His eyes darkened instantly, pupils dilating as his gaze swept over me. The intensity in his expression made my breath catch in my throat.

"Are you sure?" he asked, his voice a low rumble that I felt in my core.

I nodded, not trusting my voice. The anticipation building between us was almost unbearable.

Without breaking eye contact, Brett took my hand and led me deeper into his apartment, past the sleek living room with its floor-to-ceiling windows showcasing the glittering cityscape, toward what could only be his bedroom.

The space was minimalist but luxurious—a massive bed with charcoal sheets, ambient lighting that cast everything in a warm glow, and more of those incredible windows that made me feel like we were suspended in the night sky.

He turned to face me, his expression a mixture of desire and vulnerability.

Brett's eyes never left mine as he guided me to the edge of the bed. I sat down, my heart pounding so hard I was certain he could hear it. The city lights twinkled through the windows, casting his face in a play of shadow and light that made him look even more devastating.

"You're sure about this?" he asked again, his voice husky.

I nodded, finding my voice. "Yes. I want to see what I do to you. How you think of me when I'm not here."

Brett's jaw tightened, and for a moment I thought he might refuse. Then he nodded slowly, the intensity in his gaze making my skin tingle.

He inhaled sharply, his chest rising and falling with the effort. I could see the way his fingers flexed at his sides, like he was fighting to maintain control.

"I've never done this before," he admitted. "Not with someone watching."

The confession made my heart flutter. There was something incredibly powerful about being the first to see him this way—vulnerable, exposed, completely honest.

"I've never asked anyone before," I countered softly. "But I want to see you. All of you."

Brett held my gaze for a long moment, then nodded slowly. He stepped back, creating a small distance between us. With deliberate movements, he began to unbutton his shirt, one button at a time. I watched, transfixed, as each movement revealed more of his tanned skin, the trail of dark hair that disappeared beneath his waistband.

When his shirt finally slid from his shoulders, I couldn't help the small gasp that escaped me. Brett was gorgeous—broad shoulders, defined chest, abs that looked like they'd been sculpted from marble. But it wasn't just his physical perfection that made my mouth go dry; it was the raw vulnerability in his eyes as he stood before me, allowing me to see him.

"This is what you do to me," he said, voice rough as he unbuckled his belt. "Just thinking about you gets me hard."

The sound of his zipper sliding down made my pulse jump. He pushed his pants down his legs, stepping out of them with a grace that shouldn't have been possible in such an intimate moment. Standing before me in just his boxer briefs, the hard outline of his arousal was unmistakable.

I swallowed hard, my fingers twisting in the bedsheets.

"Every night," he said, his voice dropping to that delicious register that made my thighs clench, "I lie here thinking about what I want to do to you. What I want you to do to me."

He hooked his thumbs in the waistband of his boxer briefs, hesitating for just a moment before slowly sliding them down. My breath caught as he revealed himself fully—thick, hard, and perfect. I couldn't look away.

I watched, mesmerized, as he began to stroke himself slowly. His hand moved with practiced ease, twisting slightly at the head before sliding back down. His eyes never left me, intense and burning with desire. The muscles in his arm flexed with each movement, his breathing growing heavier. A soft whimper escaped me, and I shifted on the bed, suddenly aware of how wet I was just from watching him.

"I lie in this bed thinking about you. About how you felt under my hands. How you taste."

His voice was a low, sensual rumble that sent shivers down my spine. Watching him touch himself while thinking of me was the most erotic thing I'd ever witnessed.

A low moan escaped my lips before I could stop it. The sound seemed to affect him instantly—his hand moved faster, his breathing growing ragged as a bead of moisture formed at his tip.

"Your turn Liz," he rasped. "Show me what I do to you."

His words sent a thrill through me. My hands trembled as I reached for the zipper of my hoodie, slowly pulling it down. The sound seemed impossibly loud in the quiet room. I shrugged it off, letting it fall to the floor, revealing the simple tank top underneath.

"Keep going," Brett encouraged. The raw need in his voice set my body on fire. His hand never stopped moving on his length, his eyes burning into mine.

I crossed my arms, grabbing the hem of my tank top and pulling it over my head. The cool air kissed my skin, making my nipples tighten against the thin fabric of my bra. I heard Brett's sharp intake of breath, saw the way his hand faltered for just a moment.

"I think about you too," I admitted, my voice barely above a whisper. "Every night."

I stood, my fingers trembling slightly as pushed my leggings down my legs. Brett's hand slowed on himself as he watched me, his chest rising and falling with each heavy breath. The intensity of his gaze made me feel powerful, desired in a way I'd never experienced before.

"God, you're beautiful," he whispered.

My cheeks flushed with heat, but I didn't look away.

Reaching behind me, I unhooked my bra with trembling fingers, letting it slide down my arms. Brett's eyes darkened as he took in the sight of my bare breasts, his hand tightening around himself.

"Touch yourself," he commanded softly. "Show me what you do when you think about me."

I sat back on the edge of the bed, my heart hammering against my ribs. Slowly, I slid one hand down my stomach, past the waistband of my underwear. A soft moan escaped me as my fingers found the slick heat between my thighs.

"That's it," Brett encouraged, his voice strained. "Let me see what I do to you."

I circled my clit with my fingers, my hips lifting slightly off the bed. The intensity of his gaze on me was almost too much to bear. With my free hand, I cupped my breast, pinching my nipple between my fingers as I continued to stroke myself. Brett's breathing grew ragged, his hand moving faster on his length.

"I can't take this anymore," Brett said suddenly, his voice strained. "I need to touch you."

"Yes," I gasped, withdrawing my hand. "Please."

In an instant, he was kneeling between my legs, his hands sliding up my thighs. He hooked his fingers into my underwear and pulled them down with an urgency that made me shiver. Then his mouth was on me, hot and demanding against my core, and I cried out, my back arching off the bed. His tongue was relentless, licking, circling, tasting me with an intensity that stole my breath.

"Brett," I gasped, my fingers tangling in his hair. "Oh god."

His hands gripped my thighs, holding me open for him as he devoured me like a man starved. Each stroke of his tongue brought me closer to the edge, my hips rocking against his mouth of their own accord.

"You taste even better than I remembered," he murmured against my sensitive flesh, his breath hot and teasing.

I was already so close, wound tight from watching him touch himself.

When he slid two fingers inside me while his tongue continued its relentless assault on my clit, I shattered, crying out his name as waves of pleasure crashed through me. My thighs trembled around his head, my body pulsing with aftershocks as he gentled his touch, placing soft kisses on my inner thighs.

"I'm not done with you yet," he murmured, rising to hover above me. His eyes were dark with need, his lips glistening with evidence of my pleasure. "I want to be inside you, Liz. I need to feel you."

"Yes," I breathed, reaching for him. "Please, Brett."

He moved away from me for just a moment, reaching toward his nightstand. I watched, breathless and impatient, as he yanked open the drawer and pulled out a small foil packet. My heart thundered in my chest as he tore it open with his teeth—a move that shouldn't have been as sexy as it was, but God, everything about this man was devastating.

His hands were steady but urgent as he rolled the condom down his length. I couldn't look away from the fluid motion, the controlled power in his fingers, the intensity in his expression. There was something incredibly intimate about watching him prepare like this—practical, necessary, but somehow one of the sexiest things I'd ever seen.

"I've thought about this," I whispered, propping myself up on my elbows. "About you. Inside me."

His eyes darkened at my words, pupils blown wide with desire.

"Tell me," he rasped, positioning himself between my thighs, the blunt head of his cock pressing against my entrance. "Tell me exactly what you imagined."

I trembled, both from anticipation and the vulnerability of confession. "I imagined you fucking me. Hard. Deep. Fast."

His eyes flashed with heat as he slowly pushed forward, stretching me, filling me inch by delicious inch until I gasped, my back arching off the bed.

"Like this?" he growled, withdrawing almost completely before driving back in with a powerful thrust that made me cry out.

"Yes," I panted, my fingers digging into his shoulders. "Just like that."

Brett set a relentless pace, his hips snapping against mine with each powerful thrust. Every stroke hit something deep inside me that made stars explode behind my eyelids. I wrapped my legs around his waist, pulling him even deeper, wanting—needing—more of him.

"You feel incredible," he murmured, his voice strained with the effort. "So tight. So perfect."

"More," I gasped, my nails raking down his back. "Harder."

Something primal flashed in his eyes. In one fluid motion, he flipped me over, his hands gripping my hips as he positioned me on my knees in front of him.

The new position left me feeling deliciously exposed, vulnerable in a way that sent electric currents of anticipation through my body.

"Is this what you want?" he murmured, his voice rough with desire. "Tell me, Liz."

"Yes," I breathed, pushing back against him impatiently. "Please, Brett."

He groaned, one hand sliding beneath me to cup my breast while the other gripped my hip. I felt him position himself at my entrance, teasing me with just the tip until I whimpered with need.

"Look at you," he said, his voice filled with wonder. "So perfect. So beautiful."

I couldn't respond, could barely breathe as he began to move. Each thrust was deeper than before, hitting places inside me that made coherent thought impossible. The sound of skin against skin, our mingled breaths and moans filled the room as he took me with an intensity that bordered on worship.

One of his hands slid up my spine, tangling in my hair and pulling gently, arching my back even more. The slight sting sent a jolt of pleasure straight to my core, making me cry out with a mixture of pleasure and surprise.

"You like that?" he murmured, his voice dark with satisfaction.

"Yes," I gasped, pushing back against him, meeting each thrust with an eagerness that surprised even me. "Don't stop."

His rhythm became more urgent, more demanding, and I knew he was close. My fingers found my clit again, circling with just the right pressure as he continued to drive into me.

The dual sensation was overwhelming, pushing me rapidly toward the edge.

"Come for me, Liz," he commanded, his voice rough with need. "I want to feel you come around my cock."

His words were all it took. I shattered, crying out his name as waves of pleasure crashed through me, my body clenching around him in pulsing waves. He groaned, his rhythm faltering as my release triggered his own. His fingers dug into my hips as he held me tight against him, his body shuddering as he found his release.

We collapsed onto the bed together, a tangle of limbs and racing heartbeats. Brett pulled me against his chest, his arms wrapping around me with a tenderness that made my heart ache. I could feel his heart hammering against my back, his breath warm against my neck as we both struggled to regain control.

"That put my imagination to shame," Brett murmured against my hair, placing a soft kiss on my shoulder.

I laughed softly, the sound warm and languid in the afterglow. "Mine too."

For several minutes, we just breathed together, my back against his chest, his heartbeat steadying against my spine. His fingers traced lazy patterns on my skin, sending little shivers of pleasure through me even now.

"Stay," he whispered, pressing a soft kiss to my shoulder. Not a question. Not quite a command. Something in between—hopeful and certain all at once.

I turned in his arms to face him, taking in the vulnerability in his eyes. "Just tonight?"

His expression softened, a smile playing at the corners of his mouth. "Tonight. Tomorrow. As long as you want."

My heart stuttered. "That could be a while."

"I'm counting on it," he said, a slow smile spreading across his face as he brushed a strand of hair from my cheek.

I nestled closer, my body still humming with lingering pleasure. "Be careful what you wish for, Wentworth. I've been told I'm stubborn."

"Good," he murmured, pressing a kiss to my forehead. "Because I'm not going anywhere."

His words settled around me like a blanket, warm and secure. For once, I didn't feel the need to overthink or analyze. I just wanted to be here, in this moment, with him.

Epilogue

BRETT

In my defense, I've handled high-stakes investor meetings, near-hostile board takeovers, and one deeply terrifying Mia-pitch involving glitter cannons.

But nothing—*nothing*—prepared me for Liz waking me up at 3:41 a.m. with the words: "Either my water broke, or I peed myself—jury's still out."

I, of course, responded like a calm, capable partner.

By tripping over the hospital bag, grabbing the car keys off the nightstand, and yelling into my phone, "She's leaking something! How do I install a car seat in less than thirty seconds?"

"You had nine months—"

"Logan!"

"Okay, okay. Stay calm. Do *not* try to YouTube anything right now."

"Too late. I already tried YouTube and now I'm being yelled at by a British man named Nigel!"

Meanwhile, Liz slid into the passenger seat, casually on the phone like we weren't mid-emergency. "I'm having the baby," she said to Mia. "No, I'm calm. Brett's the one spiraling."

In my defense, I was not spiraling.

From the background, I heard Mia shout, "TELL HIM TO HURRY. I HAVE SNACKS AND A T-SHIRT THAT SAYS I DESIGNED THE BABY!"

We made it to the hospital. Liz cursed like a sailor the entire drive. I may or may not have cried when they put the little squirmy, furious bundle in my arms six hours later.

She was perfect. Small. Strong. Loud—like her mom.

Liz, exhausted but somehow still sharp, gave me a crooked smile from the bed.

"You didn't faint."

"I'm saving that for when she brings home her first boyfriend."

From the hallway, Mia's voice rang out. "If you name her Epson, I am leaving this family."

I looked back at Liz. Her hair was a mess, her hospital gown was wrinkled and slipping off one shoulder, and I had never seen anyone so beautiful.

"You still hate me?" I whispered, kissing her cheek.

"Only when you leave the toilet seat up. And maybe when you hog the covers."

Fair enough.

***

Dear Reader,

Thank you so much for reading *Hating Mr. Wentworth*! I hope you had as much fun diving into Brett and Liz's world as I did writing it—every snarky comeback, simmering glance, and wildly inappropriate office moment.

This story was a love letter to the chaos of chemistry, the sharp edge of banter, and the unexpected softness that sneaks in when two people challenge each other in all the right (and wrong) ways. Watching these two enemies-turned-lovers find their way to something real was an absolute joy—and I'm so grateful you came along for the ride.

If you enjoyed the book, I'd be thrilled if you left a review. Even a quick note makes a huge difference in helping authors like me reach new readers who love smart, spicy, emotionally satisfying romcoms.

Thank you for your support—and get ready, because there's so much more to come.

With love and a wink,

Hana York

***

Ready for More?

If you loved *Hating Mr. Wentworth*, you won't want to miss the next book in the *Don't Fall for a Billionaire* series: *Taming Mr. Donovan*.

He's a billionaire pretending to be the help.

She's a travel writer who doesn't believe in fairy tales.

And neither of them is ready for what happens next.

When Logan Donovan agrees to visit one of his company's luxury resorts, he expects sun, cocktails, and a much-needed break from boardrooms and billion-dollar deals. What he doesn't expect is to be mistaken for the resort's new "guest experience coordinator"—or for the sexy, sharp-tongued travel writer to assume he's there to cater to her every whim.

Piper thinks Logan is just a charming staffer with too much free time and unfairly great hair. Logan knows he should come clean. But with Piper looking at him like he might actually be the fantasy she doesn't believe i n... he's not ready to ruin the moment.

But secrets have a way of surfacing—and when they do, this fake staffer might just lose the only woman who ever made him wish he were someone else.

Get ready for mistaken identity, sizzling chemistry, sharp banter, and the kind of HEA that feels like a five-star escape.

Taming Mr. Donovan is coming to Amazon April 8, 2025.

HANA YORK BOOKS

Hearts on Duty Series

Sparks of Temptation

Love's Anchor

On Call for You

Investigating Desire

Falling for the Rescue

A Heart Worth Mending

Don't Fall for the Billionaire Series

Hating Mr. Wentworth

For a full list of titles, please visit Hana York's website

www.HanaYork.com

ABOUT THE AUTHOR

HANA YORK WRITES FAST-PACED, heart-pounding contemporary romance packed with irresistible heroes, strong heroines, laugh-out-loud banter, and just the right amount of spice to keep things sizzling. Her books are for readers who love grumpy men falling hard, fierce women who don't need saving, and the kind of chemistry that sparks off the page.

When she's not crafting stories full of love, tension, and toe-curling moments, you'll find her daydreaming about small-town charm, plotting ridiculous meet-cutes, and consuming an unhealthy amount of coffee. She believes in happily-ever-afters, overprotective heroes who don't stand a chance against their heroines, and that every great love story should come with a side of sass.

If you love forced proximity, off-limits attraction, sizzling tension, and romance that makes your heart race, welcome to the world of Hana York!

Follow Hana York for new releases, exclusive content, and behind-the-scenes fun! www.HanaYork.com

Find all her books here: https://www.amazon.com/author/hanayork

Follow her on Instagram: https://www.instagram.com/hanayorkromance/

Follow her on Facebook: https://www.facebook.com/hanayorkromance/

Follow her on Good Reads: https://www.goodreads.com/author/show/54826946.Hana_York

Join her mailing list here: https://www.hanayork.com/subscribe